## The Chair Was Rocking.

No one was sitting there, no one was even any-place near it, but the chair was rocking quietly back and forth, squeaking softly against the wooden floor.

James stared at it, feeling the goose bumps begin to crawl on his skin.

"M-maybe it's the wind," Mike suggested, but his voice came out in a funny kind of croak.

"Oh, sure," said T. J. Her face looked pale in the moonlight. "And does the wind make explosions too?"

The others shifted their feet nervously.

"I don't know about you guys," Pete whispered, "but I'm getting out of here."

*They thought they had it planned until every-thing flew out of control. . . .*

**Books by Constance Hiser**

Critter Sitters
Dog on Third Base
Ghosts in Fourth Grade
No Bean Sprouts, Please!

Available from MINSTREL Books

# GHOSTS IN FOURTH GRADE

## Constance Hiser

**Drawings by Cat Bowman Smith**

A MINSTREL® BOOK

PUBLISHED BY POCKET BOOKS

New York    London    Toronto    Sydney    Tokyo    Singapore

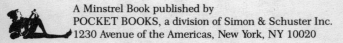

A Minstrel Book published by
POCKET BOOKS, a division of Simon & Schuster Inc.
1230 Avenue of the Americas, New York, NY 10020

Copyright © 1991 by Constance Hiser
Illustrations Copyright © 1991 by Cat Bowman Smith

Published by arrangement with Holiday House, Inc.

ISBN: 0-671-75880-2

First Minstrel Books printing October 1992

10  9  8  7  6  5  4

A MINSTREL BOOK and colophon are registered trademarks of Simon & Schuster Inc.

Cover art by Lee MacLeod

Printed in the U.S.A.

For Zoe Wommack—special grandmother,
special teacher, special friend

C.H.

For Aunt Ruth, who was always
willing to get involved

C.B.S.

# Contents

# GHOSTS IN FOURTH GRADE

# CHAPTER 1

# "I'll Get Even, Mean Mitchell!"

"You heard me!" Mean Mitchell's face was so close that James could feel the bully's breath on his cheeks. He could see the nasty gleam in Mitchell's mean, beady little eyes, too, and he knew he was in for trouble. Big trouble. "I said, get off that swing!" Mean Mitchell shouted. *"Now!"*

James gulped. Darn it! He got so tired of handing the swing over to Mean Mitchell every recess. "Now, come on, Mitchell," he began, but not too hopefully. "You know I got here first—"

3

"What's that got to do with it?" Mean Mitchell snarled. "*I'm* here now, and I said *I* want to swing! Just get yourself off there right now!"

"No," James said. "No, Mitchell, I'm not going to give you the swing. Not today."

"*What?*" Mean Mitchell jerked back as if a wasp had stung him. "What did you say to me?"

"I said—" James swallowed hard, wishing he could take the whole thing back. But it was too late now. "I said, this is one day you're not taking my swing, Mitchell!"

James figured he knew what would happen next, but at least he didn't have much time to worry about it. Because it only took a second for Mean Mitchell's big, hard fist to draw back, and then—wham! It was like those cartoons, when someone falls off a ten-story building and lands on the sidewalk with little stars dancing all around his head. Without even knowing how he had gotten there, James was lying on his back in the dust beside the swing set.

Ptooey! Something little and hard and white flew from his mouth into the palm of his hand. He stared at a big chip of tooth.

"And next time don't give me any of your big talk," Mean Mitchell ordered, plunking himself down on the empty swing. James had to roll fast so as not to get hit by Mitchell swinging over him.

Things had gotten very quiet on the playground. Looking up, James saw his friends Norman and Mike standing over him, looking worried, while Pete and T.J. came running from the jungle gym.

"Do you want me to go get Mrs. Saperstein?" T.J. asked, as the boys helped James to his feet.

James shook his head. He felt dizzy. "No, don't," he gasped. It was hard to breathe. "If we tell on Mean Mitchell, he'll kill us all for sure. I'll just sit down for a minute, and I'll be okay—"

"He's gone too far," T.J. muttered. "This time that big bully has just gone too far.

Maybe I'd better go get Mrs. Saperstein after all," she added, starting across the playground.

James sighed, sinking wearily down on the school steps. "I bet she'll make me go to the dentist. Oh—T.J.!"

T.J. stopped and whirled around. "Yes?" she called.

"Don't—don't tell her what really happened, okay?" James said. "Just tell her I fell off the swing. Well, it's the truth—sort of."

T.J. shrugged. "It's *your* tooth," she said. "I still say we ought to teach that creep a thing or two. But okay, if that's the way you want it."

She ran off, her pigtails flapping over her shoulders.

After that, the rest of the afternoon was a bad dream. By the time James's mother arrived to take him to the dentist, his mouth had begun to hurt. It felt as if someone had exploded a firecracker in there.

Lying in Dr. Arnold's big chair, waiting for his mouth to get numb, James made up his mind about one thing. "I'll get even, Mean Mitchell," he muttered. "I'll get even with you if it's the last thing I ever do!"

# CHAPTER 2

# A Terrific Idea

By the next morning, James's mouth felt much better. It was still bruised, though, and the big black-and-blue mark made him mad every time he looked into a mirror. Somehow, he thought, as he brushed his teeth—carefully—somehow, he had to teach Mean Mitchell a lesson. But how?

James had to settle for oatmeal for breakfast—his mouth was still too sore to do much chewing. That made him madder than ever—he *hated* oatmeal! By the time he had grabbed his books and his lunch box, kissed his mother good-bye, and slammed the back door behind him, all he could think about was what he would do to Mean Mitchell. If only he were just three or four inches taller and twenty pounds heavier! But he wasn't, so he would have to use his head. He would have to come up with a plan that was so smart, so sneaky, so *awful* that . . .

Suddenly James stopped in his tracks. A big smile spread slowly across his bruised-up face. Suddenly he knew exactly how to pay back Mean Mitchell.

"Do you think it'll work?" he asked his friends as they sat around the table in the lunchroom at noon. He took a tiny bit of his sandwich and chewed, being careful not to bite down too hard.

"Will it *work*?" T.J.'s grin stretched all the way across her face. "James, you're a genius, that's what you are! Ol' Mean Mitchell will never know what hit him!"

Mike and Pete and Norman weren't quite so happy with the idea he'd just shared.

"Gee, I don't know, James," Mike said, "remember what happened last time we went there?"

James snorted. "An old tree limb landed on the roof," he said. "So what? It didn't hurt anyone, did it? Aw, come on, guys—you know there aren't really any spooks in the Hathaway place."

"Oh, yeah?" Pete was so excited he was waving his bag of corn chips around, and chips were flying everywhere. "Well, that's not what my brother says—and he's in *high school!* He says *awful* things have happened in that house! He told me—"

"Yeah, yeah, I know," James interrupted impatiently. "Someone got killed there—only you notice no one ever says who or when or anything about it—and there are screams, and lights in the windows, and people go in and never come out again. We've heard it all a million zillion times, Pete. But you guys aren't going to tell me you really *believe* in all that stuff, are you?"

Pete looked grumpy as he blew through

his paper straw to make a rattling noise in his milk carton. But Norman mumbled, "I notice you never said any of that the last time. When that ol' limb fell, you ran as fast as the rest of us."

"That was before Mean Mitchell chipped my tooth," James said. "I can't believe this, guys! Do you want to take care of him or don't you?"

The boys just traded unhappy glances. Not one of them had gotten away without at least a black eye or two from Mean Mitchell.

T.J. leaned across the table. "Well, I vote with James!" she said eagerly. "Come on, tell the truth—wouldn't you really love to get even? Just a little?"

"Well . . ." Mike said at last, still not sounding too happy. But that was enough for James.

"I knew you guys weren't chicken," he said. "Now here's what we'll do. Next week's Halloween, right? We'll start tomorrow after school, at my house. I bet Mom's got a zillion boxes of old clothes and junk up in our attic.

We'll fix that old house up but good! Then we'll leave a note on Mean Mitchell's desk, see, all written up like a party invitation, and—"

"I don't know." Norman sounded doubtful. "Mean Mitchell's dumb, all right, but is he *that* dumb? Do you think he'll really bite?"

James and T.J. exchanged smiles. "Oh, he'll bite, okay," James promised. "By the time we're finished with him, ol' Mean Mitchell's going to look like the biggest scaredy-cat in the whole school!"

# CHAPTER 3

# Invitation to a Party

"This looks great, T.J.!" James opened the little square card T.J. had just handed him. It was printed with a design of black cats and orange jack-o'-lanterns, and T.J. had filled out the inside in her very neatest printing. COME TO A SPOOKY HALLOWEEN PARTY AT THE OLD HATHAWAY HOUSE, it said. BOB FOR APPLES. PLAY BLINDMAN'S BLUFF. PRIZES FOR ALL. SEVEN O'CLOCK, HALLOWEEN NIGHT. RSVP: T.J.

"I thought it looked pretty good myself," T.J. agreed. "Lucky we still had some of the invitations left over from my Halloween party last year. It looks so much better than just writing it on a piece of notebook paper or something."

"Mean Mitchell will never suspect a thing." Pete stood on tiptoe to read over James's shoulder. "This looks like a real invitation, all right." He smiled, but he still looked a little nervous.

"Now all I have to do is leave it on his desk when we go inside." T.J. chuckled. "And since he thinks I'm the one giving the party, he'll never guess that it has anything to do with your chipped tooth, James."

"That's the whole idea," James said. "He's got to think this is a real party. Boy, is he in for a surprise!"

"Cool it, guys," Norman said, out of the corner of his mouth. "Guess who's headed this way?"

Quickly, T.J. stuck the invitation back into her jeans pocket. Luckily, the bell rang just as Mean Mitchell appeared around the corner of the school building. When he caught sight of them, he grinned a nasty grin.

Never mind, James told himself, as they all lined up to march into the building. Mean Mitchell's days of grinning are just about over.

James watched out of the corner of his eye as Mean Mitchell reached his desk and saw the envelope T.J. had just dropped there. A surprised look crossed the bully's face. James figured he probably didn't get too many invitations. It took Mean Mitchell a minute or two to read the card—he wasn't exactly the fastest reader in fourth grade. Then he stuffed the invitation into the back pocket of his jeans, fast, as if he didn't want to share it with anyone. Mean Mitchell had swallowed the bait, hook and all!

Behind Mean Mitchell's back, James and T.J. traded thumbs-up signals. It was going to work! It was really going to work!

James could hardly wait for recess. He and the rest of the gang all headed for the jungle gym at the far end of the playground. Looking around carefully, James saw that Mean Mitchell was over by the swings, where he had just pushed a third-grader off a swing. It would serve the big bully right if they scared him out of his pants, James thought.

"Did you see his face?" T.J. laughed, as she hung upside down from the highest bar of the jungle gym. "I'll bet he never got invited anywhere before."

"I guess I should feel mean," James admitted, "but I don't. He's got it coming to him."

"I just hate to think what we'll have coming to *us*, if he ever figures out what we've done," Pete grumbled. "He could carve us up like a bunch of Halloween jack-o'-lanterns."

"You're not supposed to think about that part of it," T.J. argued. "Just think about how silly he's going to look running out of the Hathaway house on Halloween night. We'll tell everyone! No one will ever let him live it down!"

"Well, maybe," Mike said, looking worried

"But it still sounds really risky to me. How are we supposed to fix that old place up anyway, James?"

"I've figured it all out," James said eagerly. "I went up to the attic last night and had a look around, and I was right—there's all kinds of good junk. There are a lot of old white sheets—I thought maybe we could fix them up like ghosts, and hang them around the rooms downstairs. It'll be so dark, it ought to look really spooky. And we have a bunch of old Halloween masks, and a long black coat thing that kind of looks like Dracula's cape. We should be able to do something with all that."

"I'll say." T.J. laughed. "And I've got an idea, too—if I bring my dad's tape recorder, I bet we could make some really neat sound effects. You know, screams, and chains rattling, dogs howling, stuff like that."

Norman chuckled, and even Pete and Mike began to cheer up a little. Maybe this crazy idea was going to be fun!

"So are we all set to work at my house

after school?" James asked, chinning himself on a bar of the jungle gym.

T.J. couldn't wait, and the other boys couldn't come up with any good excuses. So it was all set—right after school, T.J. would run home for the tape recorder, and then all of them would meet at James's house.

"I can't wait to see Mean Mitchell's ugly ol' face," James said. "It'll be nice to see *him* looking scared for a change." They all had to laugh, just thinking about it.

None of them noticed that Mean Mitchell had gotten tired of the swings. None of them noticed that he had sneaked up behind them and was standing only a few feet away, behind a big old tree. None of them saw the mean gleam in his eyes as he listened to their plans for haunting the Hathaway house.

Not one of them saw his grin as the school bell rang and they all ran back toward the building. And that was a good thing—because the look on Mean Mitchell's face would have been enough to make their stomachs turn somersaults for the rest of the afternoon.

21

# CHAPTER 4

# An Afternoon
# in the Attic

"Wow!" said Mike, as the five of them stood in the attic doorway. "Doesn't your mom ever throw anything away, James?"

"Not much," James answered. "She keeps saying we're going to have a giant rummage sale someday, but that's about as far as she ever gets."

"We can do *anything* with all this junk!" T.J. exclaimed. "I mean, *look* at it!"

Boxes and barrels and big metal trunks were everywhere, sometimes piled up two and three deep. There were tall mirrors with broken frames, an old baby buggy with one wheel missing, a bent-up bike leaning against the wall. There were stacks of yellowing magazines, and broken chairs, and a couch with all its stuffing leaking out. Dust and dirt and cobwebs covered everything.

"I've piled a lot of the stuff I thought we could use over there." James pointed to the sagging couch. "But we might be able to find more in some of these old trunks." He turned toward the nearest rusty trunk and threw open its heavy lid.

A lot of the boxes and trunks held nothing but stacks of newspapers, ancient family snapshots, and scuffed-up shoes with holes in the soles. Once a mouse jumped out of a box, straight into Norman's face, making him scream and jump.

But some of the trunks held real treasures—a walking cane, the eyeless head of a big doll, long white gloves, a pair of false teeth. Best of all, in one shadowy corner, they found a headless dummy that James's mother used to use when she sewed.

23

By the time the sun began to sink and the shadows started to creep from the corners, James was so tired he ached. His back had a crick in it, there was a cobweb in his ear, and he felt as if he had swallowed about a ton and a half of dust. But it was all worth it when he saw the big pile of junk they had stacked on the couch. "I can just see it now," he said. "That old house is going to look terrific!"

"We'd better get there early Saturday morning," Pete suggested. "If we're really going to go through with this, we should get there as soon as it's light."

"Well, on Saturday, anyway," T.J. agreed. "But we *want* it to be good and dark by the time Mean Mitchell gets there on Halloween night."

"We do?" Mike asked doubtfully, but James and T.J. gave him a disgusted look, and he didn't go on.

"Let's take all this stuff out to the garage and load it on my old wagon," James said. "That way it'll be ready Saturday morning."

"We can work on our sound effects tape

out there, too," T.J. reminded them. "I think we have time before supper."

"Oh, yeah," James remembered. "I almost forgot."

"What do you mean, *forgot?*" T.J. demanded. "That's going to be the very best part!"

It took them a couple of trips to get all their junk out to the garage, sneaking down the back stairs so James's mother couldn't see them and ask questions. But finally they had it all loaded on the old red wagon, just as James's dog Tag came strolling into the garage to sniff at their sneakers and say hi.

"Tag!" T.J. greeted him. "The very person we need!"

"What do you mean, T.J.?" James asked. "I'm not so sure I want Tag mixed up in this. I don't want Mean Mitchell hurting my dog."

"He won't get anywhere near your dog," T.J. promised. "We just need Tag for the sound effects, that's all."

"So what are we supposed to be doing?" Norman asked. "It'll be dark before long, and my mother will kill me if I'm late for supper."

"Let's see . . ." T.J. looked around her. "James, could you rattle those old snow chains hanging on the wall over there? I think haunted houses all have lots of rattling chains. The rest of you can just hang around and moan and groan a lot. And I'll scream. Girls do that best. Oh, yeah—and we need to have Tag howl once in a while."

"How do we make him do that?" Mike asked.

"We could pull his tail," Norman offered, and James gave him a dirty glare. "Just gently, of course," Norman added quickly.

"Oh, no, we don't," James said. "T.J., couldn't we just forget this part? There's only one way to make Tag howl, and I—well, I don't want to do it."

"You gotta do it," T.J. insisted. "*All* haunted houses have howling dogs! It just wouldn't be right without it!"

"I'll feel so stupid," James grumbled, but by this time all the other boys were grinning.

"Whatcha gonna do, Jamesie?" Norman

asked. "Sing to him?"

James could feel his face turning red. "Well, sort of. You see, Tag—well, he always —he always howls when I—well, when I yodel."

"Yodel!" Mike exploded with a laugh. "You mean, like mountain climbers?"

"Stop laughing, guys!" James snapped. "I'm really pretty good at it. Only I guess Tag doesn't know that, because he always howls."

"Let's hear it," said T.J.

"This is so silly," James muttered, and he turned his back so he wouldn't have to look at them. Taking a deep breath, he gave a shaky "Yodel-lay-do-hooooo!"

Tag jumped to his feet. "Ow-ooooooh!" he howled, throwing his head back and pointing his nose to the ceiling.

"I can't take it," Norman moaned, grabbing his sides. All of them were red-faced from trying to hold in their laughter. Then they gave up, rolling on the floor and laughing until they could hardly breathe.

"It'll work!" T.J. said at last. "All I have to do is start the tape. We'll leave the yodeling in, too—no offense, James, but it really doesn't sound all that different from Tag's howling."

It took awhile to make the tape, but in the end they all had to admit that it sounded pretty good.

"I groan really great," Norman congratulated himself, fast-forwarding the tape to get to his favorite part.

"Well," said James, helping T.J. pack the tape recorder in its carrying case, "we've done about all we can do. Now we just have to lug all this stuff over to the Hathaway house on Saturday and get it set up."

"I get nervous just thinking about it!" Pete sighed.

"You worry too much," James told him. "This is going to be great, guys, right? I said, *right*?"

"Yeah, right," they all answered. But T.J. was the only one who sounded sure.

# CHAPTER 5

# Ghosts and Jack-o'-lanterns

James was the last to reach the gloomy old Hathaway house on that bright, sunny Saturday morning. Everyone else was already waiting outside the gate when he got there, pulling the rusty wagon with its pile of sheets, chains, and candlesticks. The dressmaker's dummy wobbled on top of the load, and down at the bottom beneath all the other junk was James's special surprise. He wasn't even going to tell the others about it—he thought he'd just wait till Halloween night and spring it on them.

"What took you so long, James?" T.J. complained, hugging her dad's tape recorder and looking impatient. The boys looked as if they'd rather be home cleaning their rooms.

"This stuff is *heavy*, you know," James said. "I had the hard part. All you guys had to do was get yourselves here."

Even James got a little quiet as they pushed open the squeaky gate and started up the long, narrow sidewalk. The closer they got, the bigger and darker and spookier the old house looked, and the louder James's heart seemed to beat.

Pete and Norman helped James drag the wagon up the sagging wooden stairs. It made a thundering noise as James pulled it across the half-rotten porch. At last they stood at the big front door. It was painted a dusty, faded black, and there was a heavy door knocker, shaped like a lion with a dull golden ring in its mouth.

"It's probably locked," Pete said.

"And it's too heavy for us to break down," Mike added hopefully.

31

"My folks would kill me if they found out we'd broken a window or anything." Norman cheered up. "Come on, guys. Maybe we ought to forget the whole thing and go home. We could play football or read comics or something."

James glared at them. "You guys sure give up easily," he said. "All those people who go in the Hathaway house and never come out again—they had to get *in* some way, didn't they? So *we* can, too. I wonder—"

He stretched his hand toward the big golden doorknob.

"You'll never get in that way," Mike argued, looking around nervously. "This place has been locked up for years and—"

His jaw dropped open as the doorknob turned in James's hand, and the door swung slowly open with a terrible creaking noise.

"You just have to use your head," James told them. "Let's go in, guys."

Inside, the Hathaway house was everything James had hoped it would be. The dark, gloomy rooms, with their high ceilings

and dust-covered floors, echoed with the sound of their footsteps. All the furniture had been covered with white sheets, and in the dim light it looked as if the rooms were filled with dozens of ghosts. Out of the corner of one eye, James caught a glimpse of something moving down the hallway, quietly and silently—and almost screamed, until he saw that it was only his own reflection in the huge, tarnished mirror that hung on one wall.

A big staircase rose from the hallway, winding around and around into the shadows above them. It was easy to imagine white shapes gliding up and down those stairs, their feet not even touching the purple-carpeted floor.

"We don't have to go up *there,* do we, James?" Pete begged, craning his neck to look up.

"No," James agreed. "If those stairs are rotten, it would be a long way to fall. I think we can scare ol' Mean Mitchell plenty down here. He won't be sticking around that long, anyway."

Somewhere in the house, a loose shutter began to bang in the wind. It sounded as if something were outside knocking, wanting to come in. Even James felt a little cold shiver on the back of his neck.

"Let's get going," he said. "No point in hanging around here all day. Let's see, we've got fifteen sheets for ghosts, and how many rooms on this floor? Did anyone count?"

It didn't take long to plant all their tricks around the house. There were "ghosts" enough for every room—two or three in some rooms—hanging from curtain rods or empty nails where pictures had once hung. They placed the dummy at the end of the hall, in front of the big mirror, with the black cape draped around its shoulders. On top of the dummy, James stuck a jack-o'-lantern he had carved the night before. On Hallow-een night, he thought, with a flashlight in-side the snarling pumpkin face, it would knock the wind right out of ol' Mean Mitchell. T.J. arranged a few flashlights here and there throughout the house—not enough to give any real light, just enough to make a nice, spooky glow. The doll's head hung from a string in the middle of a doorway—in the dark, it would look as if it were floating in midair. Even the false teeth looked gruesome, sitting by themselves on the bottom post of the stairway.

Then they rehearsed. Everyone would have a job to do. They would all dash from room to room, slamming doors, rattling chains, and being careful to stay out of sight. Norman was in charge of the tape recorder, moving around from place to place so Mean Mitchell couldn't track it down. It wasn't all that easy to move quickly from room to room without a lot of noise, but James made them keep at it until they got it right.

"It will be easier on Halloween," James told them. "For one thing, it will be dark, and we'll all wear dark clothes so we'll be harder to see. For another thing, by now we know our way around this place, and Mean Mitchell doesn't. He'll be scared out of his head."

And then there's my secret weapon, James added silently, thinking of the special surprise he had stashed behind the long velvet curtains in the hall. If all this doesn't scare him, my surprise will for sure!

It was almost noon by the time they finally left the dark old house and came out again into the autumn sunshine. But for once James didn't mind giving up a sunny Saturday morning.

It will be worth it, he thought, sticking his tongue up to feel where his tooth had been chipped. To get even with Mean Mitchell, *anything* would be worth it!

# CHAPTER 6

# Mean Mitchell Brags

"Here comes your bus," James's mother said on Monday morning. "Have fun at the party, and don't forget to bring your costume home—you'll need it for trick or treating tonight." She gave him a quick hug and ruffled his hair. James usually hated that, but today he didn't even care. After all, it was Halloween—his favorite day in the year, next to Christmas and his birthday.

And this Halloween was going to be the best one of his whole life, he thought, as he ran for the school bus, scuffling his feet through piles of red and yellow leaves on the sidewalk.

No one did a lot of work that morning. Everyone was too busy thinking about the big Halloween party right after lunch. They would bob for apples, bite doughnuts off strings, and listen to ghost stories. Who could think about things like spelling and math and history?

Even better, James and his friends over-heard Mean Mitchell bragging at recess about the big party he had been invited to at the spooky old Hathaway house. "Yessir," Mean Mitchell boasted to a scared-looking little third-grader, "it's going to be the biggest party ever. Bet you didn't even get invited. Of course, a little squirt like you would be too chicken to go in there, anyway."

"Would not!" the third grader argued, but he sounded like he was about ready to cry.

"Oh, yeah?" Mean Mitchell snorted. "Well, cluck, cluck, cluck! Bet you'd be so scared you'd cry for your mommy!"

"What a pain," T.J. snarled under her

breath. "It makes me want to punch him."

"Don't worry about it," James told her. "We're going to get even tonight, remember? By tomorrow, the whole school will have heard about what a chicken Mean Mitchell is. He'll be too embarrassed to shoot off his big mouth for a while."

"Well, at least we know he fell for it," Norman pointed out. "He thinks there really *is* going to be a party—as if anyone would invite him to a party! Almost makes you feel sorry for him."

"Not even almost," James said firmly. "All I have to do is remember that dentist."

Finally, right after lunch, Mrs. Saperstein gave up. "I can see we're not going to get any more work done today," she said. She was pretending to be stern, but she was smiling. "May as well go to the rest rooms and put on your costumes."

With a cheer, the kids stampeded out the classroom door and down the hall, their costumes under their arms.

Stuffing himself full of punch, candy corn

and orange cupcakes, James thought happily of that night. With any luck, Mean Mitchell would scare pretty quickly, and they'd all have time to go trick or treating afterward. It would be a shame to waste his neat Frankenstein costume.

Mean Mitchell wouldn't even need a costume for trick or treating, James chuckled to himself, as he watched his enemy cram his mouth with doughnuts. Mean Mitchell was ugly enough just the way he was.

## CHAPTER 7

# Waiting for
# Mean Mitchell

By the time James had eaten his supper, done his chores, and gotten dressed for trick or treating, he was beginning to feel just a tiny bit funny. Somehow the whole idea didn't seem quite as terrific now, on the spookiest night of the year, with dark shadows falling over the sidewalks and a cold autumn wind moaning through the trees. What if something went wrong? What if Mean Mitchell killed them all, or maybe just broke a few of their bones? Worse yet—he swallowed hard just thinking about it—what if all those old stories about the Hathaway house were really true? What if there really was something strange and terrible hiding in that old house, just waiting for innocent little kids to come along, so it could— Stop it! he told himself. You're too old for crazy stories like that!

But somehow, out on the sidewalk where James stood all by himself, it wasn't that easy. Even the jack-o'-lantern in his front window looked as if it were begging him to come back inside where it was safe.

The gang had agreed to meet at the Hathaway house at six-thirty, just in case Mean Mitchell got there early. And there James saw his friends, all huddled together on the sidewalk, wearing their costumes. They didn't look any more thrilled than James felt. Well, it was *his* idea, he decided. It was up to him to keep them going.

"Let's hurry," he said. "Mean Mitchell could come any minute. Gee, isn't this fun?"

No one answered, so James pushed open the squeaky gate and started up the sidewalk. At first he thought none of the others were going to follow, but then he heard them right behind him and breathed a sigh of relief.

Up the dark, uneven sidewalk, under the gloomy old trees, up the creaking steps, and across the rotting porch—to the front door of the old Hathaway house.

James didn't want to give his friends time to change their minds—especially Pete and Mike, who were looking a little sick. He just pushed the door open and stepped into the shadows of the front hall. After a minute, the others followed.

It was darker in the old house this time, and spookier. Mike gave a little yelp when a white shape fluttered in the darkness, then groaned as he recognized one of their own sheet ghosts. T.J. went quickly through the rooms lighting flashlights, but their dim glow didn't help much—in fact, the eerie shadows they threw on the walls and ceiling just made things creepier than ever.

"Did you all remember to wear dark

clothes?" James asked. They all nodded. "Good—we won't be as easy to see that way. Everybody take your costumes off and hide them here, under this couch."

"Is there any sign of Mean Mitchell?" T.J. whispered a minute later, and James went to the front window to look.

"Nothing," he said, after a minute. "Maybe we'd better get to our places now. Norman, have you got the tape recorder? Good. Don't turn it on till he gets here, and don't forget to move around a lot. And, for gosh sake, everybody, stay *quiet,* and stay *out of sight*. Got it?"

Norman grinned as he scurried off with the tape recorder, but Pete and Mike lingered in the hall, scuffing their feet on the floor. Neither one of them looked so good. "I just want Mean Mitchell to hurry up and get here, so this whole thing will be over with," Pete said, in a voice that sounded like a croak. Then he and Mike went to their hiding places.

While the others hid, James tiptoed down

the hall to where he had stashed his secret weapon behind the long velvet curtains. And there it was, on the window seat where he had left it—his special box of glow-in-the-dark face paint, left over from Halloween two years ago, and the little mirror he had brought so that he could see what he was doing. Working quickly by the glow of one flickering flashlight, he smeared the sticky stuff over his face, neck, and hands, and looked at himself in the mirror. Yeah—it looked even spookier than he remembered. In the darkness of the hall, his skin shone an eerie silver-white color. His face and hands were the only part of him that showed—his black sweater and jeans blended right in with the shadows. From a distance, he would look like just a head and a pair of hands floating around in the air!

Now all James had to do was hide behind the curtains and wait for Mean Mitchell. The curtains were dusty, and he could feel his nose prickling. He hoped he wouldn't sneeze. And he hoped he hadn't just felt a

47

*poisonous* spider running up his arm.

T.J., from her place by the front door, hissed, "Here he comes!" James's blood froze. "Oh, no, forget it," T.J. said. "They went on by. Just a couple of kids trick or treating."

For the next few minutes nobody said anything. T.J. stood and fiddled with the fringe on the curtain, peering out into the dark and getting more nervous by the minute.

"Hey, James," T.J. said at last, "what time *is* it, anyway?"

James's watch had numbers that glowed in the dark, so he was able to tell the time even behind the curtain. "It's two minutes till seven," he called softly, and T.J. gave a little sigh.

"Okay," she said, "it's not as late as I thought."

"Why rush things?" Norman muttered from across the hall. "Let's just enjoy breathing while we still can."

"Oh, be quiet, Norman." T.J. was beginning to sound a little grumpy.

James was starting to feel grumpy, too, when Mean Mitchell still hadn't shown up fifteen minutes later. "Let's give him fifteen minutes more," he said. "If he doesn't show up by then, we'll know he chickened out. Maybe he's not as brave as he wants everyone to think."

The minutes crawled by. Lost in the folds of the heavy velvet curtains, James thought he knew what a caterpillar must feel like after months in its cocoon. His skin had begun to itch under all that glow-in-the-dark paint, and he was pretty sure that a spider had begun spinning a web in his left ear.

He looked at his watch. 7:22. What if Mean Mitchell never came?

7:25. His right foot was asleep, and he thought he heard strange rustlings from the top of the curtain. Could mice climb velvet?

7:27 . . . 7:28 . . . 7:29 . . .

James sighed a deep sigh. "Okay, guys," he said, starting to step from behind the curtains, "I guess we may as well give up and . . ."

BANG!

The sudden noise in the hall behind them made them all whirl around. BANG! BANG! BANG-BANG-BANG! The noise was so loud as it echoed off the walls that they had to put their hands over their ears. Then, with a last enormous BANG, the racket ended, and the old house was quiet again.

# CHAPTER 8

# Who's Haunting Hathaway House?

"What *was* that?" James heard Pete whisper. His voice was shaky. "Something you didn't tell us about, James?"

"I don't know," James said, shrinking back behind his curtain. "Honest, guys, I don't know anything about it. Maybe we ought to—"

"Oh, my gosh," T.J. shrieked, *"what's that?"*

Nervously, James peeked through a crack in the curtains. What he saw made his blood run cold. Across the hall, in the big, gloomy living room, a rocking chair sat all by itself in a patch of moonlight. *And the chair was rocking.* No one was sitting there, no one was even anyplace near it, but the chair was rocking quietly back and forth, squeaking softly against the wooden floor.

James stared at it, feeling the goose bumps begin to crawl on his skin.

"M-maybe it's the wind," Mike suggested, but his voice came out in a funny kind of croak.

"Oh, sure," said T.J. Her face looked pale in the moonlight. "And does the wind make explosions, too?"

The others shifted their feet nervously.

"I don't know about you guys," Pete whispered, "but I'm getting out of here."

He began to back toward the front door, not turning his back on the empty, squeaking chair.

Then Norman yelled, "The light! The blue light!"

From the far end of the room, deep in the shadows, an eerie blue light had begun to flicker off and on, off and on.

"It's coming from that closet," Mike moaned. "There's something in there!"

"It's the blue light," Pete whispered. "The blue light that shines whenever someone dies in the Hathaway house! My brother told me! He said—"

"Oh, be quiet, Pete!" T.J. wailed. "And let's get *out* of here!"

But just then the closet door swung slowly open the rest of the way, making a terrible creaking noise. T.J. screamed and the boys all yelled as they saw the figure standing there—a tall, eerie-looking figure wrapped in something white. Whatever it was, it didn't make a sound—it just stood there silently for a moment, looking at them. Then, just as silently, it took a step—then two—and then it was out of the closet and gliding across the room, straight toward T.J. and the boys!

None of them ever figured out exactly what happened next. Everyone screamed and scattered across the hall. There was a lot

of noise and confusion for a few seconds. Then James heard a loud thud. Peering from behind the curtain, he saw two dark figures on the floor, both of them squirming and yelling.

"Get off of me!" That was T.J.'s voice. "I said, get *off* of me! Somebody *help!*"

"You tripped me!" complained the other voice. "No fair! You tripped me!"

That voice sounded strangely familiar, James thought. But no, it couldn't be—

Somehow T.J. managed to untangle herself from the white figure—just someone wrapped in a white sheet, James saw now. And a second later, when the sheet slipped and fell, they all saw the angry, scowling face of—

Mean Mitchell!

# CHAPTER 9

# To the Rescue!

"Mitchell!" T.J. gasped, scrambling to her feet. "What are you doing here?"

Mean Mitchell had to unwind yards and yards of sheet before he could stand up. He was looking madder and more dangerous by the minute.

"What am *I* doing here?" he spluttered, when he finally got to his feet. "The same thing all of *you* are doing here—trying to find out who's a big chicken!"

James gulped. He knew he really ought to step from behind the curtain and get between Mean Mitchell and T.J., before things got too nasty. He knew that *he* was the one who was acting like a chicken, just standing there. But somehow he couldn't make his legs move, and his hands wouldn't reach out to push the curtain out of the way. All he could do was stand there, and listen, and watch.

"You mean—you knew all along?" Norman moaned.

"The whole time." Mean Mitchell grinned his rotten grin. "The note said to be here at seven, so *I* came at *six*. I just wanted to see who it was who thought they were so brave!" He snickered. "It turned out you weren't really so brave after all, huh?"

"Mitchell Monaghan!" shouted T.J., springing at the bully, her fists clenched and her face furious. "Mitchell Monaghan! What a mean, nasty, low-down trick to play on us! You dirty rat!"

She looked like a tiny kitten spitting at a St. Bernard. Even her pigtails seemed to bristle as she yelled up in Mean Mitchell's face.

"T.J.!" Pete groaned. "Watch what you're doing!"

Mean Mitchell's mouth dropped open, and he just stood there, staring at her. James wanted to shut his eyes. What was T.J. trying to do, get herself killed?

Norman tried to grab T.J.'s arm, but she just shook him away and went on talking, louder and faster than ever.

"You ought to know better than to play tricks like that on people!" she yelled. "Do you know what could *happen?* What if someone had a heart attack or something. Mitchell Monaghan, you are the *dirtiest, lowest, sneakiest . . .*"

Suddenly she stopped, her face looking strange, as she stared at the sheet ghosts, and the dummy, and the tape recorder lying on the floor.

"Okay, okay," she snapped, "so I guess we were going to play a few tricks on you, too. But at least we had a good reason!"

"*What?*" Mean Mitchell demanded. "Why *me?*"

"Why *not* you?" T.J. shouted. "All you ever *do* is play mean tricks on people! Why do you think everyone calls you *Mean* Mitchell?"

"I don't *like* that name." Mean Mitchell narrowed his eyes to dangerous-looking slits.

Move! James ordered himself. Get out there and stop T.J. before she gets herself smashed into a million pieces. But his legs still weren't listening to him.

T.J. went right on yelling. "Well, it's a good name for you! There isn't a single cell in your whole body that isn't just plain *mean!*"

"Why, you little twerp!" Mean Mitchell snarled. He took a big step toward T.J., his hands balling into fists.

"No!" Norman shouted. "No, Mean Mitchell, you can't do it! Not even *you* would hit a *girl!*"

Suddenly James's feet came unglued from the floor. Before he even had time to think about what a dangerous thing he was doing, he snaked one hand out from behind the curtain. If he stretched, he thought, he could just reach the long black cape that was draped around the old dummy . . .

There! Thinking fast, James threw the cape around his own shoulders. It fell almost to the floor, covering everything right down to the tops of his sneakers. With any luck, Mean Mitchell wouldn't recognize him in this ghost getup.

Then, taking a deep breath, James stepped out from behind the curtain, waving his arms and trying to moan like the monsters on the Saturday-afternoon horror movies on TV.

"Ooooooh," he groaned, forcing his shaky legs to take him straight toward Mean Mitchell. "Ooooooooooowwww . . ."

Mean Mitchell swung around. James groaned to himself as he saw the fury in the bully's face. Now James had done it for sure. Mean Mitchell would probably break one and maybe even both of his legs.

Suddenly, Mean Mitchell's face changed. The mean, nasty look disappeared as if someone had rubbed it off with an eraser. His mouth dropped open, and his skin turned a funny shade of grayish-white in the moonlight.

"It's the ghost!" he screamed. "Let me out of here! It's the *real* ghost!"

For a second Mean Mitchell's feet slipped and slid on the floor, like someone trying to run in a cartoon. But then he found his footing, and off he tore, down the hall, through the front door, and out into the night. James could hear the clatter of his footsteps as he dashed across the porch and over the rickety steps.

For a moment James stared after him in amazement. He could hardly believe it—it had really worked! He laughed as he turned to his friends—but something strange was happening to them, too. They were all crowded together in a little knot, their backs pressed tightly against the wall, inching step by step toward the front door. And their faces looked just as pale and frightened as Mean Mitchell's!

"What is it, guys?" he demanded. "You all look like you saw a ghost or something."

They froze in their tracks, staring at him. "J-James?" T.J. asked in a tiny little voice.

"Of course it's me!" he yelled. "What did you think—?"

And then he got it. "Oh, you mean *this!*" He grinned as he held out one glowing hand. "Aw, come on, guys, it's just my glow-in-the-dark makeup from two years ago. Remember? When I was Dracula?"

T.J.'s face was suddenly furious again. "James," she snapped, "of all the dirty things to do! And we thought you were on our side, too!"

# CHAPTER 10

# Trick or Treat!

It took a little while for all the boys to get T.J. to calm down—once she got mad, it was hard to get her to listen to anything. But finally she looked at James with a little giggle.

"Well," she said, "I have to admit you probably saved my life. But, oh, James, you ought to see yourself—that was the scariest thing I ever saw, just a head and two hands floating in the air! You made such a *ghostly*-looking ghost."

"That was the idea," he said. "Only I didn't mean to scare you, too. I just thought it

65

would scare the pants off ol' Mean Mitchell!"

"Speaking of *him*," said Pete, "how did he do all that stuff, anyway? I don't mind telling you, when that chair started rocking, I thought there really *was* a ghost in here!"

"That's easy." Norman pointed to a string that ran from the bottom of the rocking chair to the closet where Mean Mitchell had been hiding. "All he had to do was pull on this."

"And look!" Mike showed them some beaten-up old pots and pans lying on the closet floor. "That explains that awful noise—he was beating these things together."

"But the light?" T.J. asked. "The blue light?"

James thought about it for a minute. "Oh, sure, I get it," he said at last. "He must have had a flashlight with a blue plastic bag tied over it. Remember, Pete, like the ones we used in the school play that time?"

"Well, I guess that explains the whole thing," T.J. agreed. "And now, guys, let's go home. I don't want to hang around this place another minute!"

"Me neither," Pete agreed.

It took a minute or two to gather up the flashlights, the tape recorder, and the Halloween costumes. Then the gang marched out to the front porch, breathing a sigh of relief as the door creaked slowly shut behind them.

Nobody said anything until they were a good three blocks away from the old house. There they stopped, leaning against an old brick wall, still feeling shaky. Around them, the sidewalks were full of trick or treaters, dressed like ghosts and witches and skeletons. A friendly jack-o'-lantern grinned at them from a gatepost, and they heard a little kid yell "Trick or treat!" from someone's front porch.

Slowly, they began to feel better.

"I can't wait to tell everyone at school tomorrow," James smiled happily. "Wait till they hear how Mean Mitchell ran!"

"Yeah!" T.J. laughed. "I guess you got your revenge all right, James. Ol' Mean Mitchell will never seem as scary again."

"You know what, guys?" James said. "T.J.'s right. I'm feeling better, and we've still got plenty of time to put on our costumes and go trick or treating!"

"Hey, yeah!" they all cried.

Mean Mitchell and the old Hathaway house were almost forgotten as the gang scrambled back into their costumes and headed up the sidewalk, grinning at the friendly jack-o'-lantern as they went by.

## ABOUT THE AUTHOR AND ILLUSTRATOR

CONSTANCE HISER was born in Joplin, Missouri, and received her degree in literature from Missouri Southern State College. She lives in Webb City, Missouri, with her husband and two children.

CAT BOWMAN SMITH has illustrated a number of children's books. She lives in Buffalo, New York.

# CATCH UP WITH
# JAMES AND HIS FRIENDS!

☐ **NO BEAN SPROUTS, PLEASE!**

☐ **GHOSTS IN FOURTH GRADE**

☐ **DOG ON THIRD BASE**

☐ **CRITTER SITTERS**

## By Constance Hiser

Available from Minstrel ® Books
Published by Pocket Books